COLOMA PUBLIC LIBRARY

D1625316

DATE DUE

DE 2 0 73			NY 2 1 '06	

PRINTED IN U.S.A.

OCT 3 1984   DE 16 97

JW 16 99

NO 2 3 73   DE 07 73

F

J

Clymer, Eleanor

Cly   Harry, the wild west
       horse

HARRY, the Wild West HORSE

drawings by Leonard Shortall

AN ALADDIN BOOK
Atheneum

HARRY,
the Wild West
HORSE

Eleanor Clymer

PUBLISHED BY ATHENEUM

TEXT COPYRIGHT © 1963 BY ELEANOR CLYMER

PICTURES COPYRIGHT © 1963 BY LEONARD SHORTALL

ALL RIGHTS RESERVED

PUBLISHED SIMULTANEOUSLY IN CANADA BY

MCCLELLAND AND STEWART LTD.

MANUFACTURED IN THE UNITED STATES OF AMERICA BY

FAIRFIELD GRAPHICS, FAIRFIELD, PENNSYLVANIA

ISBN 0-689-70303-1

CONTENTS

HARRY, the Wild West HORSE

Harry Loses His Job

Harry was a big brown horse. He had friendly brown eyes and a soft nose, a thick black tail that was fine for swishing flies, and a mane that waved in the breeze when he ran. He lived on the Jacksons' farm, back in the days when farmers needed horses for their work.

There was plenty of work to do on Mr. Jackson's farm, and Harry liked to do it. He was a very important animal on the farm.

He pulled the plow for Mr. Jackson. He

pulled the hay wagon, with another horse to help him.

When Mr. Jackson could spare him, he took Mrs. Jackson to town to do the shopping.

On Sunday mornings he took the family to church in the buggy, and on Sunday afternoons he sometimes took them visiting.

When he wasn't too busy with other things, he let Thomas ride on his back. Thomas loved Harry very much. He would go out to the pasture and give Harry an apple to crunch. Harry loved apples.

Then Thomas would get on Harry's back, and off they would go. Thomas wore a big hat and spurs. He liked to pretend he was a cowboy in a Wild West show. There were no television programs in those days, but there were Wild West shows that were almost as good. Cowboys set up tents in a field, and the people came from all around to see them. The cowboys did fancy riding and roping. Sometimes there were Indians dressed up in war costumes, and the cowboys and Indians chased each other.

Thomas and Harry practiced in the pasture. "Giddap!" Thomas shouted, and Harry galloped as if the Indians were after them. Thomas loved to feel the wind blow through his hair. He loved to hold on to Harry's strong neck and hear his big hooves pounding the earth. He even taught Harry some tricks. Harry could jump over a barrel, and he would stand when the halter trailed on the ground, just like a western horse. And afterward he would nuzzle Thomas's pocket for more apples.

But Harry did not have much time for play. There was too much work to do on the farm. There was so much to do that Mr. Jackson had to get started before it was light in the morning.

Mrs. Jackson cooked his breakfast by lamplight. She piled his plate with ham and eggs and biscuits to give him strength for his work.

"Seems as if I can't get the work finished,"
he said one morning. "I'd get another horse,
but where would I get a man to drive him?"

"One of these days Thomas will be big
enough to help you on the farm," said Mrs.
Jackson. "Eat your breakfast now, Thomas,
and drink your milk so you can grow fast
and help Pa."

Thomas drank his milk, but he didn't say
anything. He didn't want to let on that he'd
rather join a Wild West show.

"I can't wait for Thomas to grow," said

Mr. Jackson. "I've got to get the work done now."

The next week a man came out from town to show the farmers how a tractor worked. Tractors were new in those days. The men all gathered around the iron monster with its big wheels.

"You reckon it'll work?" Mr. Jackson asked.

Mr. Gilligan, their neighbor, said it wouldn't.

"New-fangled stuff," he snorted. "Gets

out of order all the time. Nothing like a good horse."

Mr. Gilligan was old and didn't hold with new ideas. But Mr. Jackson believed in progress. He got the tractor. It made a lot of noise and puffed smelly gasoline smoke. But it could pull the plow all day without getting tired.

"This is progress, all right," said Mr. Jackson, happily, sitting up on the high seat and working the controls.

Thomas liked the tractor because it gave Harry more time for rides in the pasture.

Of course Harry still had plenty to do. He pulled the wagon on the farm. He took the family to town. He waited patiently while they did their errands, and then he took them home again. If it rained, they had to hurry, because they didn't want to keep Harry standing in the rain.

One day, when they were slogging home in a downpour, Mr. Jackson said, "This takes

too long. I'd like to get one of those automobiles."

"Now, Mr. Jackson," said Ma, "you just bought a tractor about a year ago. You think you can afford a car, too?"

"Well, maybe not right away," said Pa.

But a few months later he decided he could. He bought a small black car.

Mr. Gilligan came to look it over. "Newfangled thing!" he said. "I don't hold with that. It'll never take the place of a good horse."

The car was nice, though. It went so fast

that they could get to town in half the time Harry took. Why, it would go twenty miles an hour! And it didn't mind waiting in the rain. And when they got home, it didn't have to be unhitched and rubbed down. It didn't need to be fed and watered.

"That's progress!" said Mr. Jackson.

Harry still pulled the farm wagon, with firewood or stones or feed.

But the next year Mr. Jackson said, "I saw a truck in town. Feller says he'll give me a good bargain. If I had one of those, I could haul a lot more at one time."

"Now, Mr. Jackson," said Ma, "don't you think we have enough machinery?"

"Well, maybe," said Pa. But a few months later he got the truck. It was big and green. It could haul a ton of rocks and not get tired. Even Mr. Gilligan thought it was pretty good.

And now, all of a sudden, there was nothing for Harry to do except give Thomas rides.

Mr. Jackson said, "I can't keep a horse eating his head off just for that. Harry's a farm horse. He ought to be working."

He tried to sell Harry. But the other farmers had enough horses, or else they had tractors, too.

"I'll lend him to Mr. Gilligan," said Mr. Jackson. "He needs a horse, and he'll at least feed him."

So Harry went up the road to Mr. Gilligan.

Harry Takes A Walk

Mr. Gilligan was old and didn't do much farming. So Harry had very little work to do. He took Mr. Gilligan to town for shopping. He took him to church on Sunday. And that was about all. The rest of the time he stood around in the barnyard, for Mr. Gilligan didn't have a pasture.

Thomas went to see Harry as often as he could. He took him apples and carrots. He patted him and talked to him and rode him up and down the road. But Harry wasn't happy. He didn't like this kind of life. He was bored.

"I wish you were my horse," said Thomas. "I'd ride you in the pasture every day." But he knew that even this would not be enough. Harry wanted to do something all the time.

One day Harry was standing in the barnyard, with his big brown head hanging over the gate. It was a warm September afternoon and he felt sleepy, although he hadn't done a thing all day. The flies tickled him, and he waved his tail and tossed his head to get rid of them. His chin itched. He scratched it by rubbing it up and down on the gate.

Suddenly his chin pushed the latch up, and the gate swung open!

Harry was surprised. He didn't know why the gate had opened. But he didn't stop to wonder. He walked out. Well! There he was on the road! Where should he go?

Down the road was the Jacksons' farm. The other way, the road went up over a hill.

That was the way Harry went.

It was nice to be out on the road. The sun was shining, and the wind was blowing, and the little birds were singing. Goldenrod and purple asters bloomed by the roadside. Harry felt happy.

"Heh-heh-heh-heh!" he whinnied, tossing his head.

Pretty soon he came to a farmhouse. He walked up to it, looking for people. But nobody was in sight.

On the kitchen window sill was an apple pie. It smelled sweet and warm. Harry opened his big mouth and—the pie was all gone. He swished his tail and walked on over the hill.

After a while he came to another farm. Some chickens were pecking in the yard. Harry liked chickens. He walked up to them.

"Heh-heh-heh-heh!" he whinnied in a friendly way.

But these chickens didn't know Harry. Squawk! They ran in all directions.

Harry tossed his head at the foolish creatures and walked on. Clop, clop, clop his big

feet went, making round hoof marks in the dust. After a rather long walk he came to another farm. Here some people were sitting in easy chairs on the lawn in front of the house. Harry walked over to them.

They were boarders, city people who had come to the country to get some fresh air. They didn't know about horses.

"Oh! A horse! He's after us!" they scream-ed. And they ran into the house.

Silly people! Harry walked on again. He began to feel hungry and thirsty. He ate some grass by the roadside, but there was nothing to drink.

At last he came to a village. On a stand in front of a store were some nice red apples. Well, if he couldn't have a drink, an apple would do. Harry reached for one. But he bumped the stand with his big nose, and the apples rolled all over the street.

"Shoo! Get away, horse!" shouted the woman in the store, running out and waving her apron.

Harry trotted away.

"Whose horse is that?" everybody asked. "Catch him!"

The village policeman ran after him, blowing his whistle. But Harry trotted on out of the village and walked into a field to take a rest.

In the field were some wagons. Men were busy unloading them and putting up tents. In one corner of the field some horses were tied.

There was one man who didn't seem to be doing anything but watching the others and giving orders. He wore a cowboy hat like Thomas's, only bigger. Harry walked up to him.

"Hello," said the man. "Who are you?"

Harry did not answer. He put his nose down and rubbed the man's shoulder.

"Where do you live?" the man asked.

Harry looked around the field, and at last he found what he was looking for—a big tub of water. He walked over to it. He put his face down into the water, right up to his eyes, and drank and drank. My, that was good! At last he raised his head. Water dripped from his face. He blew through his big nostrils and stamped his foot on the ground.

"Well, let's do something," he seemed to be saying.

"We'll have to find out where you came from," said the man. "Right now I'm too busy. But you can stay here and watch. This is a Wild West show. After the show I'll try to find your owner."

Harry didn't understand all this talk. But he liked the man with the big hat. He whinnied and pawed the ground.

"Heh–heh–heh–heh!"

The man seemed to understand him. He jumped on Harry's back. "Giddap!" he shouted. And off they went around the field.

"You look like a farm horse, but you cer-

tainly can run," said the man.

"Hey, Sam!" called one of the other men. "Where did you get the farm horse?"

Sam laughed. "He walked in here looking for a job," he said, getting down from Harry's back. "I'm trying him out."

And now the show began. A crowd of cowboys ran out of a tent. They rode their horses into the ring and began to do tricks. They chased Indians. They roped steers.

It was a good show. Harry got excited at all these men and horses galloping around, and he began to run, too. Sam jumped on his back and they raced some other horses, and Harry won. It was lots of fun.

Where Is Harry?

In the meantime, Thomas was busy, too.

All day, he had been sitting in his seat in school, but his thoughts had been far away. In his mind's eye, he saw himself riding on Harry's back, wearing a huge hat and silver spurs. He was the best rider in the outfit. He could ride hanging on to his horse's neck with one arm. With the other arm he could twirl a rope that shot out and landed around the neck of the biggest steer in the herd. What use were spelling and arithmetic? Would they help a man to ride better? The teacher had a hard time making Thomas do his work.

But at last school was over and Thomas woke up. He knew it was just a dream. He was just a boy in school, and Harry was a farm horse standing with his head over the gate, waiting for his friend. The only thing Thomas could do was try to cheer Harry up. He hurried off to see him. He didn't stop at his own house but went straight up the road to Mr. Gilligan's place.

There was the gate. But it was open.

And where was Harry? Thomas looked in the barn; he looked in the front yard; he looked across the road. Harry was not there.

"Mr. Gilligan! Mr. Gilligan!" Thomas called. "Where is Harry?"

Mr. Gilligan was taking a nap on his porch, with a handkerchief over his face. He was sound asleep and snoring.

Thomas thought it wouldn't be much use to wake up Mr. Gilligan. He'd have to find Harry himself. He put his schoolbooks down on the porch and went out into the road. Which way had Harry gone? Had he started off toward the Jacksons' farm, or had he gone the other way?

Thomas looked down at the dusty road. Yes, there were some big round hoofprints in the dust. They led up over the hill. Thomas started up the hill, too.

It was a nice afternoon for a walk. But it would have been nicer to be riding on Harry's back. Thomas had an idea.

"When I catch up with Harry," he

told himself, "we won't come home. We'll just keep on going till we find a circus or a Wild West show."

But where was Harry?

Thomas trudged along until he came to a farm. He went to the house and knocked at the door.

"Have you seen a big brown horse go past?" he asked the farmer's wife.

"No," she answered, "but I saw hoofprints in my flower garden, and somebody ate an apple pie off the window sill. Was that your horse?"

Thomas looked at the hoofprints. Yes, they were Harry's.

"I'm sorry," he said. "I'll ask my mother to make you another pie."

"Don't bother," said the woman. "Just keep your horse locked up."

"I will if I can find him," said Thomas. And he walked on over the hill, kicking a stone ahead of him to make the time pass.

At the next farm he stopped again.

"Have you seen a big brown horse?" he asked the farmer.

"No," said the farmer, "but something scared my chickens and walked all over my vegetable garden. Maybe that was your horse."

Thomas looked at the hoofprints again. They were Harry's.

"I'm sorry," he told the farmer. "When I come back, I'll work in your garden to pay for it."

"Never mind that," said the farmer. "Just take care of your horse."

"I'll try to," said Thomas.

At the next farm, he asked again whether Harry had been there.

"Yes, there was a brown horse here," said the woman in the house. "He scared my boarders half to death. Why do you let him walk on the road by himself?"

"He got out," said Thomas.

"Maybe you don't keep him busy enough," said the woman.

Thomas sighed. He knew she was right. He trudged on until he came to the village where Harry had knocked over the apples. It was getting late in the afternoon, and Thomas was tired. He was getting discouraged, too. Would he ever find Harry? He looked around and saw the village policeman standing next to the fruit stand.

"Excuse me," he said, "but did you see a brown horse walking around loose?"

"He was here," said the policeman. "He knocked over this fruit stand and spilled all the apples."

"Which way did he go?" Thomas asked.

"Off that way," said the policeman, pointing.

"I've got to find him," said Harry. "But I think I'll rest a while first." And he sat down on the curb in front of the store. His feet hurt and he was hungry. But where could he get anything to eat? Suddenly he had an idea.

"Could I have some of those apples Harry knocked down?" he asked the woman in the store. "I'll pay for them as soon as I can get some money."

"You can have them free," said the woman, "only you'd better catch that horse of yours."

"I wish I could," said Thomas wearily.

The policeman looked at Thomas closely. He was dusty and hot.

"Where do you live?" the policeman asked.

"Way back over the hill," said Thomas. "I've been walking all afternoon, and I still haven't found Harry."

The policeman looked surprised. "You mean to tell me your Pa sent you out by yourself to find that horse?"

"Oh, no!" said Thomas. "He doesn't know about it. You see, he doesn't need Harry. He lent him to our neighbor Mr. Gilligan. But Harry doesn't like it at Mr. Gilligan's. And Pa doesn't want a horse eating his head off and doing nothing around the farm. So I'm going to find Harry, and we'll get a job in a Wild West show. Do you happen to know where there is one?"

"Yes, I do," said the policeman. "One went through here today. It's in a field out-

side of town, same direction your horse went. Maybe you'll find him there."

"Wow!" said Thomas. "You really think so? I'd better go!" And he jumped up and hurried out of the village, munching an apple.

Just beyond the last houses of the village, he saw some tents in a field.

"That must be it!" he said to himself, beginning to run.

People were coming out of the field. The show was over for the day. Thomas ran faster.

There were the horses over in a corner. Men were carrying water to them. There were spotted horses, black ones, grays, and roans. And there was a big brown horse drinking out of a tub!

"Harry!" Thomas shouted. "I've found you!"

The Wild West Show

Harry lifted his head. The water dripped out of his mouth and splashed back into the tub.

"Heh-heh-heh-heh-heh!" he whinnied happily, trotting up to Thomas. He stamped his big forefoot and nuzzled Thomas's shoulder, pretending to bite him.

"Have an apple," said Thomas, holding one out in his hand. Harry crunched the apple with his strong teeth. He walked over to a fence and stood beside it so that Thomas

35

could get on his back. Thomas climbed up, and Harry trotted across the field. He looked over his shoulder at Thomas.

"See this nice place I found!" he seemed to be trying to say. "It's great! It's just what we want."

The tall man in the big hat came over to them.

"My name is Sam," he said. "Is this your horse?"

"Yes, he is," said Thomas. "I'm Thomas Jackson, and the horse is Harry. How did you find him?"

"He just walked in here," said Sam. "I was going to look for his owners after the show, but now I won't have to. Can you ride him home?"

"Of course I can," said Thomas, "but I don't want to. There's nothing for Harry to do at home, and he doesn't like it. Pa lent him to our neighbor Mr. Gilligan, but he just keeps him in the barnyard all day. So if you'll give me and Harry a job in your Wild West show, we'll work for you and we can be together."

"You want a job? How old are you?"

"I'm ten, and I'm strong," said Thomas. "I can carry water, and I can feed the horses and rub them down. I can ride, too. Want to see me?"

"All right," said Sam. "Let's see you ride."

"Giddap!" said Thomas. He hung on to Harry's neck and they tore around the field, raising a cloud of dust where the grass was worn away.

"How was that?" Thomas asked, stopping in front of Sam.

"Pretty good!" said Sam, nodding thoughtfully.

"And that's not all," said Thomas. "Harry can jump over a barrel. And he will stand when the reins are dragging. I never learned to rope a cow because Pa wouldn't let me, but I could learn. If I'd known you were here, I would have brought my cowboy hat and my spurs."

"That's all right about the hat," said Sam. "But what about your Pa and Ma? Are you sure they'd want you to go off with a Wild

West show?"

"Well, I don't know," said Thomas. "I didn't think about that. But I'll tell them that Harry is happy, and I think they'll understand. I can write them a letter."

"And what about Mr. Gilligan?" Sam asked. "What will he do without a horse?"

Thomas was not worried about Mr. Gilligan.

"My Pa will be glad to give him a lift to town or to church," said Thomas. "I don't think Harry needs to stand around all week just for that. You can see he's better off here."

Sam nodded. "You're right about Harry," he said. "But I'm not so sure about you."

"I'd be all right if I had something to eat besides apples," said Thomas. "Have you got any food? I don't have any money, but I'll be glad to work for it."

"Why, yes!" said Sam. "You come with me."

He took Thomas over to the chuck wagon.

"Hi, Red," he said to the cook. "Fix this hand up with a plate of chow."

"Yes, sir!" said the cook. "Is this a new hand joining our outfit?"

"I don't know yet," said Sam. "We've got to do a little figuring first."

Thomas sat down on a rock and ate the beans and bread and drank the coffee that Red gave him. It all tasted very good. He was sure he'd like working here. He bit into a big slab of pie and sighed with relief.

Suddenly, as he munched the pie, there was a loud chugging noise and a cloud of dust at the gate. A small black car came roaring into the field. There were three men in it.

Sam walked over. "Hey, mister," he said to the driver. "You'd better leave your machine over there. You'll stampede the horses if you drive it in here."

The driver paid no attention. He was excited about something. "I'm looking for a boy about so high and a big brown horse," he said.

"Why, it's Pa!" said Thomas. "Come on, Harry, we'd better go talk to him!" And he ran to the car, with Harry following at his heels.

"Hello, Pa!" said Thomas. "Hello, Mr. Gilligan. How did you find us?" Then he saw that the third person in the car was the policeman. "Oh, did you tell my Pa where to find me?"

"Yes, he did," said Pa. "I've been asking at every farm on the road. Mr. Gilligan saw your books on his porch, and we followed your tracks in the dust. What's the idea of going off like that without telling anybody? Your Ma is sick with worry."

"She is!" said Thomas.

"Of course," said Mr. Jackson. "This is the first time you've done such a thing, so I won't say too much. But if it happens again, I'll whale the daylights out of you. Get in the car."

"But, Pa!" said Thomas. "Wait! Let me explain. Harry and I, we can get a job in the Wild West show. Then Harry will be happy,

and I can be with him. Just let me go home and get my cowboy hat and spurs. Then Ma will see that I'm all right."

Pa looked at him. "What's all this?" he demanded. "A job in a Wild West show?"

Sam explained. "The horse walked in here by himself this afternoon," he said. "I was going to look for his owners as soon as the show was over. But then this young feller walked in, too. Seems he was looking for the horse. When he saw our outfit, he asked

44

for a job and I was just about to talk it over with him. Now, Thomas, I'd like to have you. But I can't use any more hands under fourteen years old."

"You can't?" said Thomas, very disappointed. "I'd work for nothing, if you'd feed me and Harry."

"But how would you go to school?" Sam asked. "This outfit travels around a lot."

"Do I have to go to school?" Thomas asked.

His father nodded. "I'd let you off," he said. "But your mother would never agree. I'd never hear the last of it. Why, I wouldn't have a minute's peace. And what's more, she'd want to know if you brushed your teeth and said your prayers every night, and wore your rubbers when it rained, and if you were drinking your milk every day."

Thomas sighed. He thought about the coffee and beans he had had. He was sure his mother wouldn't like his drinking coffee. And he was sure Sam wouldn't like one of his

45

hands to have his mother come asking if he brushed his teeth and wore rubbers.

He looked up at Sam unhappily. "I guess it wouldn't work out," he said. "All right, let's go home. Come on, Harry."

Thomas Decides

Thomas started to climb on Harry's back, but Pa stopped him. "I don't want you riding him all that way," he said. "Tie him to the car and get inside."

Thomas tied Harry's halter to the back of the car. But Harry didn't like that. He rolled his eyes and reared back.

"Whoa, boy, easy there!" said Thomas. "Pa, I guess I'll have to ride him."

"I'll guess you will," said Pa, in a worried

voice. "I'll go slow, and you follow me. Don't let Harry get out of hand."

"Harry doesn't like automobiles," Thomas explained to Sam.

"Can't say as I blame him," said Sam. "I'm in favor of horses, myself. But automobiles are here to stay, they say."

He watched Thomas get on Harry's back. Suddenly he said, "Wait! Maybe we can make a deal after all."

"What kind of a deal?" Mr. Jackson asked. "Hurry up, I've got to get the milking done."

"Seems as if I could use another horse," said Sam. "You want to sell this horse?"

"Well, I don't know," said Pa. "I did want to sell him, but my neighbors had all they needed. Seems as if the horse would be happy with you."

"We try to keep our horses happy," said Sam. "This horse has been well trained. He can run fast, and he'll stand when the reins are dragging. He's nice and friendly, not

mean. He's never been trained for roping, but I figure he could learn. What do you say?"

"Well, if it was just me, I'd sell him," said Mr. Jackson. "But Mr. Gilligan here needs a horse to get to church and to town. Of course, we can always give him a lift."

Mr. Gilligan spoke up. "Got a surprise for you, Jackson," he said. "Heh, Heh! I've been making a deal with a feller that wants to sell me a car!"

"Gilligan, I thought you were against new-fangled doo-dads," said Pa. "What's got into you?"

"Progress," said Mr. Gilligan. "I got tired of hitching and unhitching. Besides, I can't stand to see that horse of yours looking so unhappy when I'm not using him. Figure a car will stand in the barn till I get good and ready to take it out, and won't need no rubbing down and feeding either."

"Well, Gilligan, that's a surprise," said Mr. Jackson. "But I want to tell you one thing. A horse has sense enough not to run into a tree, but if you're driving a car you

have to have sense enough yourself."

"That's a true fact," said Mr. Gilligan. "Now hurry up and tell the man if you're aiming to sell or not, and let's get on home."

Thomas had been listening to all this talk. He looked from his father to Sam. Would his father really sell Harry? He put his face against Harry's warm coat. If Pa did sell Harry, he might never see him again. If Pa didn't, Harry would go on doing nothing. Either way was terrible, but waiting was worse. Why didn't Pa decide?

Suddenly he heard his father say, "Well, Thomas, what do you say?"

Thomas lifted his face from Harry's coat. All the men were looking at him.

"About what, Pa?" he asked.

"It's up to you, Thomas," said Pa. "Do you want Harry to stay here with Sam, or do you want to take him back home again? I'll leave it up to you."

Thomas stared at his father. Such a thing had never happened before. Pa always decided things in the family. What was the matter with him?

"Up to me?" Thomas said.

"Yes," said Pa, nodding. "I figure you know what's best for Harry, and I'll do what you say."

"You mean, if I say *no*, you won't sell him? And if I say *yes*, you will?"

"That's right," said Pa. "Only hurry up,

because I've still got the milking to do, and your Ma is wondering what's become of us."

Thomas looked up at Harry. He thought of him galloping around the ring in the Wild West show, happy and busy. Then he thought of him standing in Mr. Gilligan's barnyard, doing nothing, with his head hanging down.

And he thought of himself, never riding on Harry's back any more. Could he stand it? Well, maybe he could.

"I've decided," he said. "Let Harry stay here."

All the men looked at him—Pa, Mr. Gilligan, Sam, and the policeman.

"You sure?" said Pa.

Now it was Thomas's turn to be impatient. "I said I decided!" he exclaimed. "Come on, let's go home."

All he wanted now was to get away, be-

cause if he stayed much longer he was afraid
something terrible might happen. He might
cry!

Sam stuck out his hand. "Shake, Pard-
ner," he said. "You won't regret it. We'll
take good care of Harry."

"He—he likes apples," said Thomas.

"He'll get apples," said Sam.

"Th-thanks," said Thomas, climbing into
the car.

Pa got out, said something to Sam about
settling the deal, and cranked the car. It gave

a loud roar, and there was a burst of blue smoke from the rear. The car shook as though it might fall apart. Pa ran around and jumped in. He took off the brake, and the car bounced forward.

Harry jumped back. Then he saw that Thomas was leaving him. He started to follow, but Sam took hold of the halter.

"Wait!" Sam shouted. "I've got something more to say!"

Pa stopped the car, but he didn't turn off the motor. He didn't want to get out and crank again.

"What is it?" Pa shouted.

"Any time we're in the neighborhood, you can come to the show, free!" Sam shouted back.

Thomas smiled. "I can?" he said. "Thanks!"

That was better. That meant it wasn't forever. The Wild West show would come back. He would see Harry again. Maybe when he was fourteen, he could even join the show. Meanwhile, he didn't really want to leave home. The sun was setting. Soon it would be dark. It would be nice to be home, eating supper at the kitchen table.

He watched Sam lead Harry away. Sam was talking to the big brown horse and patting him.

"So long, Harry," said Thomas.

Then he turned around in his seat. "Come on, Pa," he said. "Let's get the milking done."